To my beloved son **Seth** and husband **Sinan**

-S.A.

Can Do It!

ISBN 978-0-578-97615-0 (paperback)
978-0-578-99960-9 (hardcover)
978-0-578-31589-8 (ebook)

www.SarinaAbbasi.com

❀

First Edition

Can Do It!

written by SARINA ABBASI illustrated by SUPUNI S.

I am a **can** who can't.

Have you ever heard of such a thing? A can who can't?
I know it sounds silly, but that's me!
I'm a can who can't do **ANYTHING!**

I just **CAN'T!**

It wasn't always
this way.
I haven't always
been a can who
can't.

When I was a little can, I could.
I was a **brave** little can -
I loved to try out **new things!**

But then,
a **bad thing**
happened.

I had a **shiny** new bicycle, and it was the first
time out without my training wheels.
I got myself up on the seat and
started to pedal.
"Can do it! Can do it!"
shouted my family from the sidewalk.
I was flying! Wheeeeeeeee!!
But then.....

CRASH! I really was flying - over the handlebars and onto the sidewalk!

CRRRRUMMMP!!

I landed with a terrible thump! It hurt so badly, and - oh, no! - I had a big dent in my shiny, smooth metal!

I'd even started to leak, just a little.

NOOOOOOO!!

My folks were **so kind**.
"It's okay to fall down!"
they said.
"Every can falls
sometimes,"
they told me.
"If you get back up
and **keep trying**..."
they suggested.

But it was too late.
I knew right then that I would never
be a can who can.

Not like my friends...
They can do **all sorts of things**
that I just...can't!

Some of my friends can play soccer.
They can run **super-fast** and **score** a gazillion goals!
They don't even have to try! **They just can.**

I went to watch them play.
They looked like they were having heaps of **fun, zipping up** and down the field.

They **cheered** each other on,
"Come on, you can! Yes, you can!"
"GOOOOAAL!!"

I **wished** I could join in,
but I'm just a can who can't.
"Come join us!"
one of the players shouted.

"I'm no good at
soccer," I mumbled,
"I **can't** do it!"

"Baloney!"
one of them scoffed.
"You can, if you just
give it a try."

"We all had to **practice**
a lot to get this good,"
another one said.

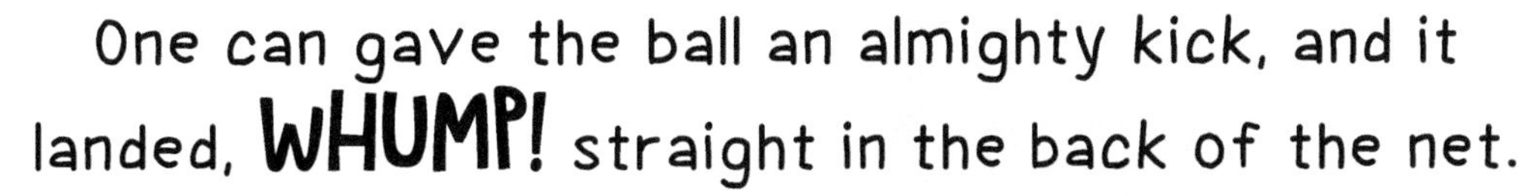

One can gave the ball an almighty kick, and it landed, **WHUMP!** straight in the back of the net.

"You don't understand..." I tried to explain, "I'm not like you cans who can. I. Just. Can't."

And I slumped away, feeling **very sorry** for myself.

I think you've got to be born with
talent like that! They just can.
I went to watch their band practice.

"TWWANGGG!"
the ukuleles
thrummed
together.
"PLLINGGG!"
the tunes tangled,
so prettily!
Every now and then somebody
played the wrong note...
but they just carried on like
nothing had happened!

"Would you like a go?" offered one of the cans, holding out her ukulele.

I **shook** my head, "Oh, no! I'd just ruin it for everyone!"

"Hey, **no problem!**" she smiled.
"Everyone's gotta start somewhere..."
She was **such a kind** can, but I'd run away already.
Why? Because I. Just. Can't.

I know cans who can do **taekwondo**.
They can kick like **rodeo horses** and punch like **bears!**

I don't think
they even find it **hard!**
They just can.
I went to their taekwondo training session.
They were the **strongest**, **coolest**
cans I had ever seen.

"Haaiiiy-A!!"
they shouted together.

"Kiiii-hup!!"
they hollered.

One by one they knocked each other down,
clattering and **scattering** across the mat.

One can waved to me.
"**Your turn!** Show us what you've got!"
"Don't **waste** your time," grunted his friend,
"this can won't try anything!"

I was so **ashamed** that I could feel
myself shrinking inside.

"But I'm different from you! **I. JUST. CAN'T!**"
I started to run, embarrassed and sad to be the can who can't.

Running home,
huffing and puffing and
trying not to cry,
I rounded a corner.
In the street was a can I'd never
seen before, riding a scooter.
Suddenly - SLAM!!
He hit a storm drain and crashed down
on the asphalt! He began to cry.

I rushed over to him. "**It's okay**, little can! Ouch, that looks like it hurts!"

He had a dent in his side, fresh and sore-looking. I pointed at my dent and smiled.

"It won't hurt forever, I promise! After a while you won't even know it's there."

I **helped** him back onto his scooter and he rode away, still **sniffling** a little.

And as I watched him disappear, I realized something really important. I just helped that little can do exactly what everybody tells me I should be doing - trying again!

If that little can could do it, then maybe... just maybe...

I could do it too...?

Nowadays, I **try new stuff** all the time! And you know what? If it doesn't go quite right, I **always** try again.

Sure, I still fall off my bike sometimes. I even leak every now and then, too - but I can always **patch** myself up.

I'm still not great at
soccer, but playing
is so **incredibly fun**
that I don't even care!
I'm **getting better**
all the time.

My ukulele playing is
pretty bad, really - but I just
start the song **again!**
I **keep on trying** and I
always get there in the end.

I may not kick as high as the other cans in taekwondo, but every lesson **I learn** something new!

I'm **getting closer** all the time.

The **best part** is, I really didn't have to change much at all to try these fun new things.

All I had to do is **remind myself** that, actually, I...

Can Do It!

CPSIA information can be obtained
at www.ICGtesting.com
Printed in the USA
BVHW052002041221
623133BV00001B/2